Clickety Clack

To our family, with appreciation for all your love, support and guidance.
Special thanks to Dewey Bergman, Jr. —R. S. and A. S.

To my husband, Ken, and my son, Batman (Matthew).
I love you with all my heart. —M. S.

ISBN 0-439-16577-6

12 11 10 9 8 7 6 5 4 3 2 1   0 1 2 3 4 5/0

Printed in the U.S.A.   08

First Scholastic printing, October 2000

Set in OptiAdrift

Clickety Clack

by Rob and Amy Spence

illustrated by Margaret Spengler

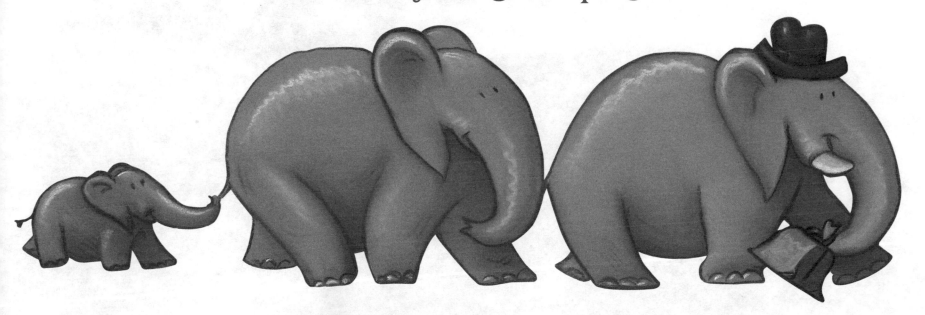

SCHOLASTIC INC.

New York Toronto London Auckland Sydney
Mexico City New Delhi Hong Kong

A little black train goes down the track.
Clickety clack, clickety clack.

A red caboose is in the back
Of the little black train going down the track.
Clickety clack, clickety clack.

The cars are full of talking yaks,
And a red caboose is in the back

Of the little black train going down the track.
Clickety clack, clickety clack.

Seven tumbling acrobats
Sing on the cars with talking yaks,
And a red caboose is in the back

Of the little black train going down the track.
Clickety clack, clickety clack.

A troupe of ducks goes quack quack quack
While dancing around the acrobats
Who sing on the cars with talking yaks,

And a red caboose is in the back
Of the little black train going down the track.
Clickety clack, clickety clack.

Elephants stomp in two big packs
And the troupe of ducks goes quack quack quack
While dancing around the acrobats

Who sing on the cars with talking yaks,
And a red caboose is in the back
Of the little black train going down the track.
Clickety clack, clickety clack.

Two mice light fireworks...

BOOM and CRACK!
And then . . .

"Keep it down!" yells Driver Zach.
"You're giving me a headache attack!
If you don't pipe down, we'll change our tack.
We'll stop going forward ... and we'll head right back."

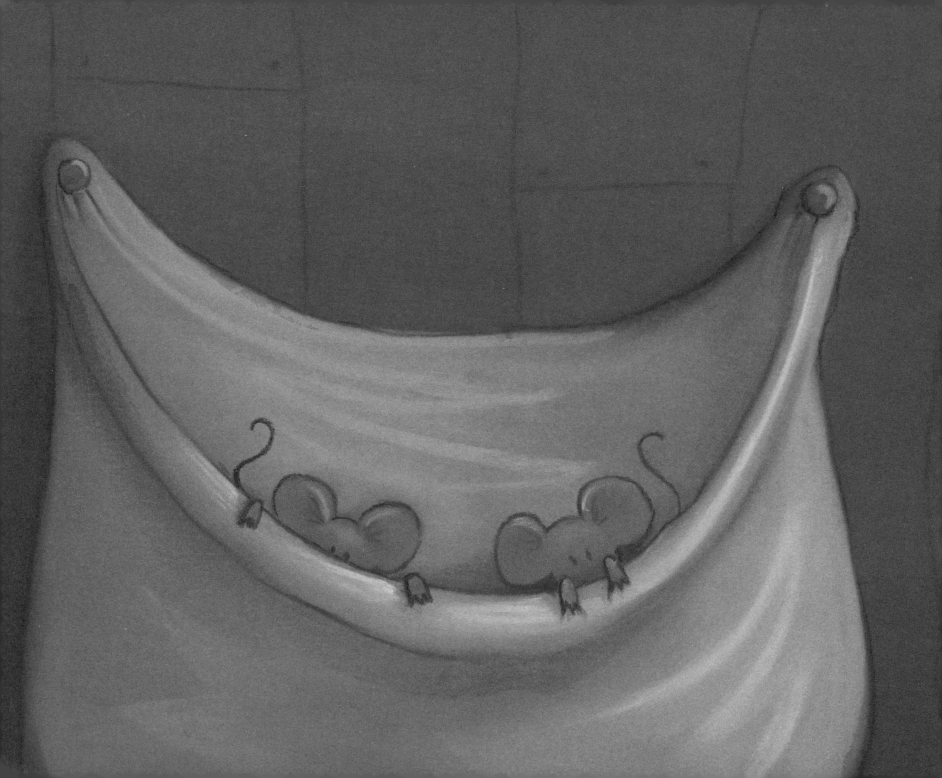

So the mice both jump in one big sack
As elephants rest in quiet packs,

And the ducks all stop their quack quack quack

With no sound at all from the acrobats

Who sit on the cars with silent yaks.
And a red caboose is in the back

Of the little black train going down the track.

Clickety clack, clickety clack.

A smile's on the face of Driver Zach.
And the only sound you hear, in fact,
Is the sound of the wheels on the railroad track.

Clickety clack, clickety clack.